that's SO raven

Raven's So Gold Guide to Life

Based on the series created by

Michael Poryes
Susan Sherman

DISNEY PRESS

New York

That's
so me!

Text by Heidi Hurst

Printed in the United States of America
First Edition
10 9 8 7 6 5 4 3 2 1
ISBN 0-7868-4662-3
Library of Congress Catalog Card Number 2004105553
For more Disney Press fun, visit www.disneybooks.com
Visit DisneyChannel.com

What's up?

    I'm Raven. But hey, you probably already knew that! I know, I know . . . my style is fierce. Fashion's my thing! And wait until you check out my <u>So Gold Guide to Life</u>. You are gonna love it! I'm going to spill everything about my crazy life! Of course, I can't tell you all of my secrets, because, you know, a girl's gotta have some mystery. I'm also going to tell you all about the important things in my life, like boys, fashion, shopping, boys. . . . Oh, snap, I already said that. Think your life is insane? Then check out mine!

Love ya,

Raven

ALL About Me!

I'm a totally normal teenager who just happens to be psychic. My very best friends in the world are Eddie and Chelsea, who've always got my back, even when I'm wrong. I love going to school, which is crazy I know, but there's always something fun going on.

Life at home is full of excitement, too. My parents are pretty cool, and my annoying little brother, Cory, is always there for me to make fun of.

Most of the time, I just chill in my room, working on my fashion. I make all of my own clothes, so I can be totally unique. But I also love to shop, especially for shoes. I am crazy about shoes. Hmm, I wonder if the mall is still open. . . .

THE BARRACUDIAN

PSYCHIC FREAK WALKS AMONG US

BARRACUDAS

Can you imagine if the school newspaper printed this?

My Visions

I've been psychic all my life. I get it from my grandmother Vivian. Sometimes I feel like she's the only person who can really understand me. I keep it a secret from the people at school because I don't want to feel like a freak. It's hard enough to fit in, just imagine if everyone knew my secret!

Vision quest!

	So Gold ✔	Not So Gold ✗
Place to be:	Hangin' at The Chill Grill 	Front row of Lawler's class (He spits, eww!)
Fashion statement:	The more colors, the better	School uniforms, yuck! 
How to treat your friends:	Always listen to them	Ditch them for cool kids
Talking to cute guys:	Flirt and make eye contact 	Drool and trip over your feet
Getting a good grade:	Team up with the smartest kid in class	Steal the test and tell your friends the answers

Hey Dad!

My dad, Victor, is a professional chef who also owns his own restaurant, The Chill Grill. It's great to have a chef as a dad because something always smells good in the kitchen. My dad's not too strict, and he's always cracking jokes. Sometimes he's a little out of control with the crazy outfits, but he makes me laugh.

That look has got to go, Dad!

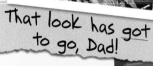

Mom and Dad are gettin' down!

Check him out!

Scary Halloween!

The Chill Grill

Tonight's specials

Baxter Beef Stroganoff

❖

Potatoes à la Victor

❖

Kool Key Lime Pie

Kapowee!

Hey Mom!

My mom, Tanya, used to be a teacher, but now she devotes all of her time to Cory and me. She says raising us is a lot harder than being a teacher. Once she was my substitute teacher. I was so embarrassed, but she totally understood and turned down a full-time job at my school. How cool is that? My mom is my best friend, though, and we love hanging out—watching chick flicks, going to a spa, or shopping.

Mom=Teach
How embarrassing!

Pass me a hanky!

This was the coolest day ever! Mom and I got to meet my favorite singer, Maisha, at a spa.

Mom & Dad's Secret Past

Psst . . . before they had me and Cory, my mom and dad were a singing group called Toast & Jelly. They wore really funny old-school outfits and sang cheesy R&B songs. They even appeared on a talent show, Soul Search.

My Bro' Cory (or as I sometimes call him, maggot!)

My little brother Cory exists to annoy me. He's always doing things like putting bologna in my CD player—eww—or licking the phone receiver before handing it to me. C'mon now, that's just nasty.

Cory sure does think he's all that. He likes to walk around flexing his nonexistent muscles for Chelsea, because he's so in love with her. But she thinks he's a pesky little brat . . . which he is.

Oh, puh-leeze!

Poor Chelsea has to fend off Cory every time she comes over.

$$ \$ \$ \$ $$

I don't know what Eddie was thinking when he made Cory his manager. Cory booked him a gig rapping for senior citizens!

In your dreams, Cory!

Cory's Crazy Cash Schemes

My brother is cheap. He's always looking for some insane way to make money, and he saves every penny. Try to get a loan from the kid, and you'll get shot down. Trust me, I learned that a long time ago.

My mom and dad were <u>sooo</u> mad when Cory opened up a credit card in the name of his rat, Lionel. He was out of control shopping with that card.

I don't know how he does it, but Cory's safe is more secure than the Federal Reserve! Here's a picture of me getting snagged by one of his booby traps.

raven's *rules* 🚶🚶🚶

How to Deal with Irritating Little Brothers

Get a lock on your bedroom door, so he can't get to your stuff.

. Get your own phone line, so he can't listen to your conversations.

. Do NOT let him know who your crush is, because he will use it against you.

4. Find out who his crush is and use it against him.

5. Keep him away from your friends, or he might get a crush on one of them.

Once Cory sold all of the furniture from our house to raise money to buy a new video game. Mom and Dad were <u>not</u> happy.

My Girl Chelsea!

Chelsea Daniels is my girl, for real. We've been best friends for as long as I can remember. Some people, like Mrs. DePaulo, say that Chelsea is my sidekick and that I boss her around. That is so not true! Okay, maybe I did blow out the candles on her fifth birthday cake, but she was taking <u>way</u> too long making that wish.

Chelsea stole Gomez, a rival school's mascot, to try to save him.

Chelsea loves her dog, Sam, so much that she freaked out when a guy named Sam asked her out. I mean, would you date a guy that had the same name as your dog?

Sometimes Chelsea goes a bit overboard loving those trees.

Chelsea's parents are therapists, so she knows how to solve any problem. She totally helps me figure out all the drama in my life. She's also really into animal rights and the environment. I think she'd save every animal in the world if she could. She's super concerned about global warming and stuff like that. But she is totally down with my hobbies, too—like shopping!

Save the crabs!

Queen Chelsea

Chelsea's Likes

1. Saving animals and the rain forest
2. Recycling ♻
3. Talking on the phone—to me!
4. Flossing: the girl's gotta have clean teeth
5. Camping △

Chelsea's Dislikes

1. Eating meat
2. Hurting people's feelings
3. Trying to be like everyone else
4. Keeping secrets
5. Getting bossed around

My Boy Eddie!

Eddie Thomas and I have been friends for as long as I've known Chelsea. Now, I know we'd make a cute couple and all, but that is so <u>not</u> gonna happen. We are just friends, and that's it. Okay, once I made him pretend to be my boyfriend to impress my cousin, but that was really weird.

Eddie's life is basketball. Since he made the team, he's been obsessed with playing. It's cool, though, because every game gives me an excuse to check out the hotties on his team. He's also a talented rapper, and we give him props every time he thinks of a new rhyme.

Good lookin' out, Eddie!

My boy is Starting Guard for the Bayside Barracudas!

After Cory stole his clothes, Eddie got him back with a whipped cream assault. Snap!

I try to help Eddie with girls as much as possible. He's always going through some sort of dating drama, like when his girlfriend Andrea accused him of being a clown, and then caught him being a real clown at a birthday party. Or one time, he got a huge pimple before a big date. I tried everything, even some facial treatments, but nothing would get rid of that thing! Finally, I covered it (perfectly, if I may say so) with concealer.

raven's rules 🎎

ow to Have a Guy Best friend

- Be interested in things he's into, like basketball. Sports always come first.

- Be willing to go out on a limb for your boy— even if it means embarrassing yourself in front of your crush.

- Be honest with him when it comes to his crushes. If you think the girl is wrong for him, tell him.

Poor Eddie—Loca is loco!

Wanna know Eddie's biggest problem? She's named Loca. She's got a huge crush on him, and is always punching his arm. Talk about big bruises!

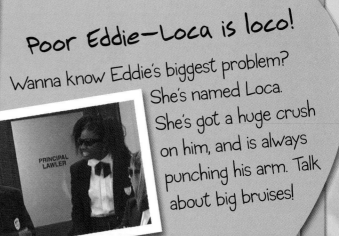

My Wacky Teachers!

Mrs. DePaulo

Mrs. DePaulo is my science teacher and she's pretty cool. Even though science is <u>so</u> not my best subject, Mrs. DePaulo makes it fun. She's also way into opera. Mrs. DePaulo is the most honest teacher I've ever had, too. She'll always tell you exactly what she thinks.

Mr. Petracelli

I have to admit that I'm a little scared of Mr. Petracelli. Students call him the Terminator because he's such a hard teacher. He also does this really weird neck popping thing that freaks everybody out. During the holidays, he's a mall Santa Claus—go figure!

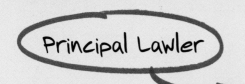

Principal Lawler

Hmm... Principal Lawler. How should I say this? He spits... like a camel! And I mean, he really spits on people. He doesn't realize he's doing it, but if you stand too close or sit in the front row when he teaches a class, you get showered. It's so nasty, but he's a really nice guy. Now that he's been promoted from teacher to principal, I don't see him that much anymore. And I'm not complaining, if you know what I mean!

How to Impress Your Teachers

✓ Make them think you're really excited about the project, even if you'd rather get your tooth pulled.

✓ Compliment their outfits, even if they are _so_ last year.

✓ Partner with the smartest person in class to get a guaranteed A.

Bayside

Good ol' Bayside is where I spend most of my time.
I may not be the most popular girl in school, but I am well-liked . . . I
think! Eddie, Chelsea, and I always seem to get into trouble at school,
like the time I had a vision of the answers to Eddie's Spanish test.
I didn't want to, but he begged me to tell
him the answers. Finally, I gave in. But at the
last minute his teacher changed the test! If
he failed his midterm, he would have been
kicked off the b-ball team. Chelsea and I
<u>had</u> to tell Eddie the answers were wrong,
but the only way to get him the message
was to pretend to be window washers.

one of the hazards of b
a window washer—pigeo

   So, there we were outside the
classroom window on a platform, trying
to get his attention. It worked, but Chels
and I were totally busted by the principal
for that one! Hey, that's what friends
are for, right?

We were
trying to do a
good thing for
Eddie, I swear!

This is where Chelsea and I have our most important discussions.

Eddie and I deejayed the school radio show! Watch out world—here we come!

KUDA

Things in my locker

Might see a cutie!

My favorite tunes

Devon's my boy!

You never know when you'll need to pretend to be someone else—I should know.

You always gotta look fly!

In case I feel like knitting during study hall.

I always gotta have my music!

I'm Stylin'!

Fashion is my life. It really is. As long as I can remember, I've totally been into making my own clothes, and I'm pretty good at it! Everyone always comments on my original outfits. Maybe in the future I'll have my own clothing line and everyone will be wearing my designs. Hmm . . . I wonder what I'll call my clothing line. Styles by Raven? Rant & Raven? The possibilities are endless!

Here's me with my mannequin in my room.

My Favorite Accessory!

I love flowers. They add that special something to my outfits.

My Fashion No-no!

I was so over this outfit before I even put it on. A stylin' teenager's outfit should never match her grandmother's!

Countdown to My All-time Best!

5. I love purple!

4. It's fake. Chels would die if I wore a real fur!

3. Who says uniforms have to be boring?

2. Check out the jacket— it doubles as a handbag.

1. My finest creation!

Surviving Alana

Alana, the biggest snob in school, has hated me since fourth grade when I was chosen to play the Tooth Fairy and she was chosen to play Tooth Decay in our school play. Hello? We were nine! Get over it already!

Anyway, she is nothing but mean to me every day at school. She has two annoying tagalongs, Loca (the arm puncher) and Muffy, who both worship the ground she walks on. I try my hardest to be nice to her, but she just ends up hating me more. It's useless!

Here's Alana talking to my crush Devon. Hate her!

I tried to save Alana from being hit with a cart in school, but it accidentally knocked her down and then paint spilled on her head instead. My bad!

Hangin' with Alana

Bonding with the "Baddies."

Sometimes Alana and I do get along. Like when we rebelled against the school uniforms Principal Lawler made us wear. We ended up in detention, but Alana thought I was cool. I even ditched Eddie and Chelsea to hang with the "bad girls."

Then, Alana wanted me to put a huge cheese that they'd stolen in the heating vents at school and blame it on Eddie and Chels. Before the heat came on, I realized I needed to get rid of the cheese. I crawled through the vent and ate it all. It was so gross. And I realized that Alana was just plain mean. I'm so glad Eddie and Chelsea forgave me!

Chelsea and Eddie didn't have my back, so I thought I didn't need them! Big mistake.

Eww, eww, eww. Not my best moment.

raven's rules
Beat Bullies!

1. Remember that your friends love you no matter what anyone else says.
2. Kill them with kindness. If they still hate you, then they've got issues that you can't cure, honey!
3. Don't stoop to their level. Calling them names back or playing pranks is only going to get you detention.

I'm in Love!

I like boys. Cute boys, tall boys, athletic boys . . . I like all types. Check out all the boys I've dated (or sort-of dated or at least crushed on)!

Ricky

Eddie's friend Ricky is so sweet and cute. One Saturday I even ditched my mom at the movies to hang out with him in another theater. But my conscience got to me, and instead of going out to dinner with him afterward, I decided to stick with my fam. Oh, but it could have been magic!

Kwizz

I had a vision that Kwizz, a supercute new guy, was going to bring me flowers. Then I saw him playing his saxophone at school. I decided I wanted to take him to the San Francisco Jazz Festival, but first I needed to earn cash. So I got a job at a psychic hotline. Believe it or not, Kwizz called in! I fooled him into thinking he needed to meet me. It was all good until he showed up at my house with flowers . . . and his <u>girlfriend</u>, Lisa. Snap!

I had the biggest crush ever on Gabriel. When he finally asked me to the school's Renaissance Dance, I was thrilled. The thing was, I also said I'd go to the dance with Ben "Stinky" Sturky because I felt sorry for him. It turned out that Gabriel only asked me to the dance because <u>he</u> felt sorry for <u>me</u>. Oh, how ironic!

Gabriel

Devon

I love Devon Carter. He was my boyfriend for a short-but-blissful time. I'd known him for a while, but he used to be pimply faced and not so cute. When he turned up after summer break as a hottie, I was totally crushing. And he liked me, too! We dated, and I even survived his psychotically jealous little sister, Nadine. Even though he moved to Seattle after his dad got married, I still think about him!

How Embarrassing!

At the school carnival, I totally wiped out by the dunking booth. Luckily, not many people saw it. But I totally ruined my superfly outfit.

Embarr-o-meter
1   10

Wipe out!

Embarr-o-meter
1   10

Butter fingers!

I'm not really sure what possessed me to jump behind the counter at the movie theater concession stand. I guess patience isn't my best quality. I'm just bummed that I ruined a perfectly good pair of boots because I didn't think to unplug the butter machine. Duh!

Fallin' for Devon!

It was my first date with Devon and I wanted everything to be perfect. He brought along his little sister, Nadine, and I dragged Cory to the pizza place, too. Too bad Nadine totally had it out for me. She beat me with the whack-a-mole mallet when no one was looking and tricked me into sitting on a slice of pizza!

Devon never saw her be mean to me, and I couldn't tell on her because he wouldn't like me anymore. I was determined to stick it out because I had a vision of Devon and me kissing. By the end of the night, I got my kiss, and Nadine earned a tiny bit of respect for me—or at least she learned to tolerate me!

Royal mortification!

Chelsea was queen at our Renaissance Dance and totally went overboard. When I accidentally "insulted" her, she ordered me into the stocks. Hello? Stocks do not go with any outfit.

Self-esteem Check!

I love to sew!

Everyone who knows me knows that I have great self-esteem, but one horrible incident made me feel completely worthless. Total trauma. When I read in <u>Teen Look</u> magazine about a contest for teen designers to model their own creations, I knew I was destined to win. My designs were hot, and I had the perfect catwalk attitude: sassy and confident. I modeled my gorgeous dress for <u>Teen Look</u>'s editor and she loved it. I thought she loved me, too. In the next issue of <u>Teen Look</u>, I was in the magazine! But the magazine put my head and dress on the body of a super-skinny model.

Here's that mean magazine editor.

At first I was a little upset, but then I began to feel really horrible. I knew I didn't have the body of a typical model, and this made me think that no one would ever let me be on the catwalk. <u>Teen Look</u>'s editor even asked me to make a smaller size of my dress for another model to wear.

Who's that girl?

Then, I got this crazy idea that I needed to lose a bunch of weight so that I could model my dress. I even got on my dad's exercise machine, but that was a complete disaster.

The day of the fashion show I finally realized that the Teen Look people were wrong. I have a great figure. I crashed the fashion show in my own dress (totally upstaging the superthin model in my design), and took over the catwalk. I was a hit!

Bad idea!

No one can keep me from my moment in the spotlight!

raven's rules

Be Yourself!

1. Wear clothes that make you feel comfortable. No one looks good when they're constantly fidgeting in their clothes.

2. Show off your favorite feature. Love your locks? Wear 'em down.

3. Hang out with friends who like you for you, not how you look.

4. Share a joke with your best friends. Laughing makes you feel so much better, plus a smile is the best accessory!

5. Look in the mirror every day and marvel at how wonderful you are.

Gotta Get That Cash!

Chels and I are so stylin'.

I am not one to miss out on a good time, so when my teacher scheduled a ski trip, I just <u>had</u> to go. But Chelsea and I had one little problem: we didn't have the money to pay for it.

Instead of asking our folks for the money, we decided it was time to get responsible. So, we asked my dad for jobs waiting tables at The Chill Grill. But here's the deal: waiting on tables is much harder than it looks, and hello, work gets in the way of chatting with my girl.

To make a long story short, Chelsea and I got fired. We felt really bad, and I knew my dad was disappointed. We asked him to give us one more chance. Luckily, he can't resist our charms. But when Chelsea and I both scheduled private parties at the restaurant for the same night, we were in so much trouble.

It's a good thing my dad bought us skis as a surprise gift, 'cause they came in handy.

One party was full of elderly ladies and the other party was for tough biker guys. They obviously didn't get along. Not to mention the third party of the night, a birthday party for Cory's friend. You know I love a challenge though, so we combined all three parties into one. We even made poor Eddie dress up as a clown to entertain the kids. (Can you believe Cory is actually scared of clowns?)

So, Chels and I, armed with the craziest idea ever—a ten-foot pizza—made the parties a huge success. My dad was so proud of us. We even used the new skis he bought for us to spread the sauce around. We got to go on the trip and it was so cool!

Eddie, quit clownin' around! Ha!

Dad said we were totally great servers!

raven's rules

First Job Dos and Don'ts

Do
Get a sensible job, like waiting tables in a restaurant.

Don't
Get a silly job, like at a psychic hotline.

Do
Save your money for a trip with friends.

Don't
Spend it on a boy, like Kwizz, that you don't even know.

Do
Have respect for your boss.

Don't
Throw a temper tantrum.

Me, Jealous? No Way!

My entire life I have been at war with my cousin, Andrea. She thinks she's so sophisticated just because she's traveled all over the world and lives in Paris. So, when I found out she was visiting, I wasn't exactly jumping for joy, you know? I decided that this time, I was going to outcool her. When Andrea arrived, I told her all about my exciting life as captain of the cheerleading squad (don't ask!). I also told her I had a boyfriend. One big problem though, I told her my boyfriend was Eddie—even after I had a vision of Andrea kissing him!

For my last show-off trick, I told Eddie, Andrea, and my family that I wanted to cook a fabulous seafood dinner. But since I can't cook, I sent Chelsea to pick up the dinner. When she showed up with live crabs, the trouble started. One of the crabs ended up grabbing strands of both Chelsea's and my hair—ouch!

This is all Chelsea's fault!

The future lo-
fine for Edd

We tried to hide it from Andrea, but she learned the truth. I was so embarrassed that I ran to my room. Andrea followed me to talk, and instead of arguing, we had a heart-to-heart. She confessed that she was actually jealous of me and my "regular" life. So, my cuz and I have been tight ever since. Oh, and because I had come clean about Eddie, he got his kiss from Andrea after all.

Andrea wanted to talk it out.

It's all good!

☺ raven's rules ↑↑↑

Green with Envy? Get Over It!

There's nothing worse than being jealous of a friend or sibling. You don't want to deal with silly drama with your friends, but sometimes it's hard to hide your jealousy. Here's how to deal:

1. Figure out why you're really jealous. The reason is usually deeper than you'd think, or at least that's what Chelsea's therapist parents always say.

2. Make a list of all the great qualities— and stuff—that you have. Your clothes, gadgets, sense of humor . . . see, you're blessed!

3. Have a heart-to-heart with the pal you're jealous of. Maybe your pal is jealous of you, too!

4. Get over it and move on. Being jealous of someone isn't going to help you get along with them, so it's time to make peace with the situation.

It's Cool to Be Nice

You know why it's so cool to be a sweet person? Because not only do other people think you're the best, but it makes you feel good about yourself, too. I know, because one of the nicest things I've ever done is befriend Ben "Stinky" Sturky. See, the kids at school call Ben "Stinky" because he has seriously nasty body odor. I guess he doesn't believe in deodorant or showering daily—or monthly for that matter.

Anyway, Ben and I were assigned to be partners in science class. I tried to ditch him, but after I had a vision of Ben and I getting an A, I decided to hold my nose until our project was done. Plus, he told me I was the prettiest girl in class, so you know, I had to give him credit. Ben and I worked on our project at my house, which made my parents pretty unhappy. Do you know how long it takes to get b.o. off a couch?

P.U.!

Ben is so smart, and I knew we'd get an A.

Mom and Dad tried to get us to work on the project at Ben's house . . . nice try.

C'mon, Ben, get clean!

Ben and I totally aced our project, and I was so happy. We buddied up at the school carnival. I ran the dunking booth and he was the dunkee. I even put detergent in the water to get him clean and soapy when he fell in. But man, no one could get him to fall in the water, until I accidentally dunked him.

Then I came clean with Ben and told him he had a problem with body odor, and you know what? He didn't even know it! Ben is such a nice guy that it doesn't matter if he's a little stinky. Ben said he'd try to shower more often. Being sweet earned me Ben's respect, and it won me a new friend!

Ben totally appreciated my honesty.

☺ raven's rules ↟↟↟

Nice/Not so Nice

Dying to know if you're a sweetheart or a snob? Here's a quick rundown of things that are nice, and things that are just not . . . so nice.

Nice

Giving your mom flowers
Telling your parents "Thanks"
Tolerating your annoying little sibling
Telling your friend, "I've got your back"

Not so Nice

Giving your mom a headache
Telling your parents they embarrass you
Locking your annoying little sibling in a box
Talking behind your friend's back

Avoid a Party Disaster #1

It seems like great party ideas are always followed by party disasters. I had the best party planned, but when this girl I can't stand named Nicki planned hers for the same night, I was doomed. She isn't a nice girl, but she is the most popular girl in class, so everyone wanted to go to her party.

I couldn't wait to get her back for this!

Plus, Nicki told the whole school that I moved my party up a week, so while I was hanging around my house in a face mask and bathrobe, the whole school unexpectedly showed up at my door. I vowed revenge on Nicki.

The next Saturday, while her party was raging down the street, I lured Nicki to my house, where we messed up her hair with a leaf blower and covered her in hair spray and leaves. We'd planned to broadcast the whole thing to her party. But my conscience took over and I helped her clean up. I sent her back to her party with a bouquet of flowers to say I was sorry, but I forgot to tell her the flowers had poison ivy in them. Oops!

Revenge is so sweet!

Oh, snap! My bo

Avoid a Party Disaster #2

After I had a vision of Cory telling me he hated me, I was freaked out. I mean, he annoys me, but I still love the little toad. What else was a big sister to do then but give her brother the best birthday party ever?

Oh no! Mom and Dad being sick totally messed up Cory's party plans.

Mom, Dad, and I were going to take Cory and his friends to the zoo, but Mom and Dad got food poisoning. I couldn't bear to cancel the party, so I phoned up Reptile Rick, who wrestles snakes for parties, to see if he could save the bash. He finally showed up, but after eating the leftovers that gave Mom and Dad food poisoning, he got sick, too!

eptile Rick, don't eat that!

I did what I do best—improvised. I dressed up as Reptile Raven and paraded around with an iguana and a snake, two things I hate! But I was totally busted when I wrestled a stuffed snake—that's when Cory's friends really knew I was a fake. The kids were just about to leave, and Cory was about to tell me he hated me, when Reptile Rick's pig had babies. The kids went crazy. Nothing like baby piglets to save a birthday party!

Reptile Raven to the rescue—crikey!

Busted!

Be a Good Friend

I think I'm a pretty good friend. I would do anything for Eddie and Chelsea, and I have. But I'll never forget the time I almost lost Chelsea as a friend for being too supportive.

our faulty ceiling made Chelsea want to run for president.

Chelsea was fed up with how nothing seems to get fixed at our school, so she decided to run for class president. She had cool ideas, and I thought she had a great chance. But then I had a vision of the results, and her opponent, Ben Sturky, had won in a huge landslide.

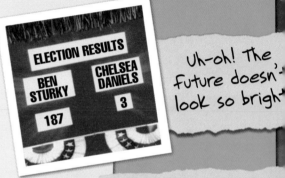

Uh-oh! The future doesn't look so bright

I couldn't let that happen. After fellow students promised they'd vote for Chelsea if I did something for them, like walk their dog or babysit, Eddie and I were swamped with voters' chores. We were able to hide it from Chelsea, until she came over and caught us in my kitchen, surrounded by animals and kids (this whole favor thing was out of control!).

The nerve of this girl wanting me to walk her dog for a vote! So, why did I do it?

At this point, I knew I had gone too far with this favors-for-votes thing.

Chelsea accused me of bribing students to vote for her. She was so mad. I guess I was bribing people, but I really wanted my girl to win.

Thankfully she forgave me and gave a great speech at the election rally. Even though Chelsea still lost to "Stinky" Sturky, who promised to stay away from people if they voted for him, it wasn't as big a loss as I'd seen in my vision. I still think she would have been an awesome president.

Chelsea didn't know the whole school could hear her telling me why she wanted to be president. They loved her ideas!

The Falling Out

Once, I started hanging out with some students who really understood me—they were psychic, too. But when Eddie and Chelsea caught me sneaking around with my new friends, I felt like I had to choose. My new friends were mean to Eddie and Chels, and even though they knew what I was going through with my psychic powers, I couldn't leave behind my two best friends. I'm so glad that's over!

These are the people I almost ditched Chels and Eddie for.

raven's rules

How to Be a Fun Friend

1. Plan activities you both love. (Eddie, Chelsea, and I love to go bowling.)

2. Be a good listener when your friend needs to vent.

3. Don't talk behind your friend's back.

4. Make a pact to be completely honest, no matter what.

5. If your friend has a crush, do what you can to get them together.

Be Cool to Your Parents

When <u>Hello, San Francisco</u> asked my dad to cook live on the show, he was so excited ... until he had an attack of nerves and wanted to back out. It was his big chance to be famous, so I faked a vision that he had a successful show. I knew he would do a great job, so what's the problem, right?

Did those two dorks really think this would work?

Well, Cory and his friend, Miles, who had a crush on me, tried to hypnotize Chelsea and me to make us fall in love with them. We were supposed to fall asleep upon hearing the words "San Francisco" and wake up at "Okeechobee." It totally didn't work—on Chelsea and me. But Dad watched the whole thing, and <u>he</u> became hypnotized, right before the TV crew showed up!

Uh-oh! Dad, wake up!

Miles had run off, and we couldn't remember the wake-up word, so Mom and I had to prop Dad up on an ironing board and try to cook for him. It was a big mess and the show's host was so mad. Finally, we found Miles and he woke Dad up. In the end, Dad wowed the host and did great. See, I knew he'd be slammin'!

Mom and I did our best to make it look like Dad was cooking.

The TV host offered Dad a monthly segment on <u>Hello, San Francisco</u>.

Share the Love

Once, I had a vision that my dad told my mom they had to "split up." So, Eddie, Chelsea, Cory, and I re-created Mom and Dad's first date at Rusty's Bar and Grill. It was a country bar, so we went all-out with cowboy costumes. I even sang a honky-tonk song.

Mom and Dad wanted to know why we went to so much trouble so I told them about my vision. They were shocked and said there was no way they'd split up. They'd been arguing because Dad lost his wedding ring in the house. When Dad said they should "split up," he meant that he would look upstairs and she would look downstairs for the ring. Oh boy, was that vision wrong! Whew!

I'm so glad my parents aren't splitting up!

I thought Mom and Dad were finished with each other.

☺ raven's rules 🕺🕴🕺

How to Get Along with Your Parents

1. Tell them you love them, and try to hug them a lot, too. They love that!

2. Listen to their advice—they know what they're talking about.

3. Make time to hang with them. If Mom wants to spend a day with you, it's because she misses you.

4. Tell them "please" and "thank you." 'Rents don't respond to rude.

5. If you're going to pester your sibling, do it when your parents aren't around.

Cowboy Cory, yee-hah!

I think I'll stick with pop music.

Be a Super Sleuth!

I always have to know what's going on. Some may call that nosy, but I prefer to call it "concerned." When I sensed that Eddie and Chelsea were keeping a secret from me, I had to find out what it was. It was also the opening of my dad's restaurant, The Chill Grill, so you know whatever my buds were doing behind my back had to be cool. At school, Eddie and Chelsea told me they had plans—together. I asked them what their important plans were and they told me they were going blurfing—bowling on a surfboard. Okay, I know there are a lot of extreme sports out there, but I'm pretty sure blurfing isn't one of them.

I had a vision of Eddie and Chelsea standing way too close to each other, and they looked like they were about to kiss. So much for blurfing! Eddie and Chelsea couldn't date—I wasn't about to be a third wheel. Then in Mr. Grozowtski's class, I spied Chelsea and Eddie swapping a note. When Eddie passed the note back to Chelsea, it landed on the floor, and I almost got it. But guess who got to it first?

I could just picture the next X Games lineup: Skateboarding, Motorcross, Surfing, Wakeboarding, Blurfing.

Whoa, what is going on here?

That secret note better be for me!

Yeah, Mr. Grozowtski grabbed it and tossed it in the trash can. I wasn't about to let that note get away, so when he wasn't looking I dug through gross garbage and got it. Chelsea and Eddie were going to meet at her house after school because they had to wait for the plumber.

What else was I supposed to do but dress up as the plumber and eavesdrop on Eddie and Chelsea? I saw enough to know that <u>something</u> was going on, and when the real plumber arrived, I got out of there quickly.

When Chelsea and Eddie showed up at The Chill Grill opening night, I confronted them again and told them I knew what they were up to. But when I found out they were just practicing a salsa dance for the opening night show, I was so embarrassed. I can't believe I thought they were dating!

The lengths I will go to discover the truth!

Hey, they've got some pretty good moves.

raven's rules

The Snoop Scoop

If anyone knows how to butt in without looking like they're butting in, it's me. Here are my tips on how to snoop around.

1. Don't be afraid to get dirty. It's a dirty job and you have to do it.

2. You've got to have a good disguise.

3. Practice different voices—in case you have to pretend to be someone else (like your mom!) on the phone.

4. Don't let your friends know you're spying on them, they hate that.

5. Don't crack up! Laughing will give you away in a heartbeat!

The Three Musketeers!

My Lucky Thirteen

13

Chelsea and I dressed up like basketball players so we could come up with a nickname for her crush, Sam. Sam had the same name as Chelsea's dog, and she couldn't stand the thought of her crush and her dog with the same name. Totally creepy. Sneaking into b-ball practice was Eddie's idea (thanks a lot, Eddie). We weren't the best players, but we had fun. Then, the coach split us up—I was "skins" and Chels was "shirts." Cool, I thought, until I realized that "skins" meant shirtless. Chels and I jetted out of there <u>real</u> fast! We never did get a nickname for her boy, but it didn't matter since he turned out to be a real, well, dog.

12 After Chelsea, Eddie, and I were photographed with Santa Claus while we were supposed to be in school, I had to go back and get the picture. It was up for everyone to see, including my parents! I got the picture, and they never knew I skipped. I can't believe I got away with it! Go me!

11 Once, I went out with an older guy, even though my parents told me not to. When they showed up at the same restaurant, I freaked out. I was supposed to be at home with Cory, not out on a date! Before I knew it, the entire restaurant staff started dancing, and somehow I ended up in the middle. Since my dad is up for anything, he started dancing, too! I had to hide from him, so I came up with this nifty little disguise. The disguise worked . . . at least until my mom caught me near the bathroom!

10 I know I look ridiculous in this outfit, but I was supposed to be a TV psychic, after all. The glasses have got to go.

Sneaking onto the basketball court **9** in the school's barracuda mascot costume was the only way I could think of to tell Eddie he had to lose the game. If he scored the winning basket like I'd predicted, snob Serena would have told the whole school I was psychic, because she overheard me talk about it earlier. I looked so silly.

8 '70s night at The Chill Grill is so much fun. I loved dressing up in this funky outfit. It is so diva-licious!

7

Here's the deal with this. I had a vision that Devon was going to kiss me. Behind him, I saw the pizza place entertainment show. On our actual date, Captain Pepperoni, the pirate animatronic, broke. The rest of the shows were canceled—and that meant no kiss with Devon. There was no way I was going to let that happen. So I dressed up as the pirate and performed in the show. I looked totally stupid, but Devon thought it was sweet. The kids got their show . . . and I got my kiss!

6

Science and I do not get along. Let's just say there was an incident with a chemistry project. The Smurf look is so not me.

5

Cory and I actually had to work together to get out of the dentist's office. There was no way either one of us was going to let the dentist tell us we had a cavity. We will do anything to avoid the drill!

4

When I accidentally got my dad fired from his job, I dressed up as the ultimate diva pop star to get his job back. It didn't exactly work, but I had fun doing it!

3

Mr. Petracelli wanted to talk to my mom about my talking back in history class (so I was loud and obnoxious sometimes . . . who isn't?), but I didn't want to tell her. He had never met my mom, so I dressed up in this oh-so-crazy outfit to meet with him. To be fair, my mom is way more fashionable than that!

2

I had to dress as Chelsea's plumber to find out what she and Eddie were doing behind my back. It's too bad I left her bathroom in worse condition than when I found it. Obviously, plumbing is not going to be a future career for me!

Mr. Carter (Devon's dad) was about to get married and move to Seattle. Somehow I had to tell Mr. Carter he couldn't just leave and take my boy with him. I didn't get a chance to tell him before his wedding ceremony, so I had to tell him during the ceremony . . . at the altar! Yes, it was a bad idea, but I had to do it! I crashed the wedding and told Mr. Carter that I didn't want Devon to leave. Devon still moved, but he'll never forget that stunt!

raven's rules

Do-it-yourself Disguise

It's totally easy to come up with a quick disguise with things you have around the house.

1. Mom or Dad's clothes come in handy when you need a new "look."

2. Sunglasses and a hat work wonders—plus, how could all the celebs be wrong?

3. Use pillows under loose clothes to make you look bigger than you are.

4. Need a cheap wig? Use a clean mop!

5. Use a funky shower curtain or colorful sheets for an instant glamorous gown.

Later!

So are you laughing, or what? Yes, my life is insane, but it's fun, too! Great friends, cute boys, and, if I may say so myself, hot fashion! If only I could control those nutty visions! But you know what? I wouldn't change a thing! I hope you enjoyed my So Gold Guide to Life and maybe you even learned a thing or two! I hope to see you again really soon!

Love ya,

Raven